Speci Little Sea Horse

written by Anne Giulieri
illustrated by Omar Aranda

"Can we play today?"
asked Little Sea Horse.

"Yes," said Father Sea Horse.
"Come on!
We will go over to the coral
where the sea horses play."

Father Sea Horse
and Little Sea Horse
went over to the coral.

They saw Spotty Sea Horse
playing in the coral.
She was going in and out
of the coral.
She was going
over and under it too.

Spotty Sea Horse
was having lots of fun.

"Look at Spotty Sea Horse,"
said Little Sea Horse.
"Look at the stars on her crown.
Her crown is so big,
and her crown is so shiny too!"

"Oh, dear!" said Little Sea Horse.
"My crown is not big,
and my crown is not shiny.
Spotty Sea Horse will not want
to play with me.
She will not want
to be my friend."

"Little Sea Horse,"
said Father Sea Horse.
"Look at your special tail.
It is long, and it is strong.
It is a very special tail."

Little Sea Horse looked at her tail.
It looked long,
and it looked strong.

"Yes," said Little Sea Horse.
"My tail is very special."

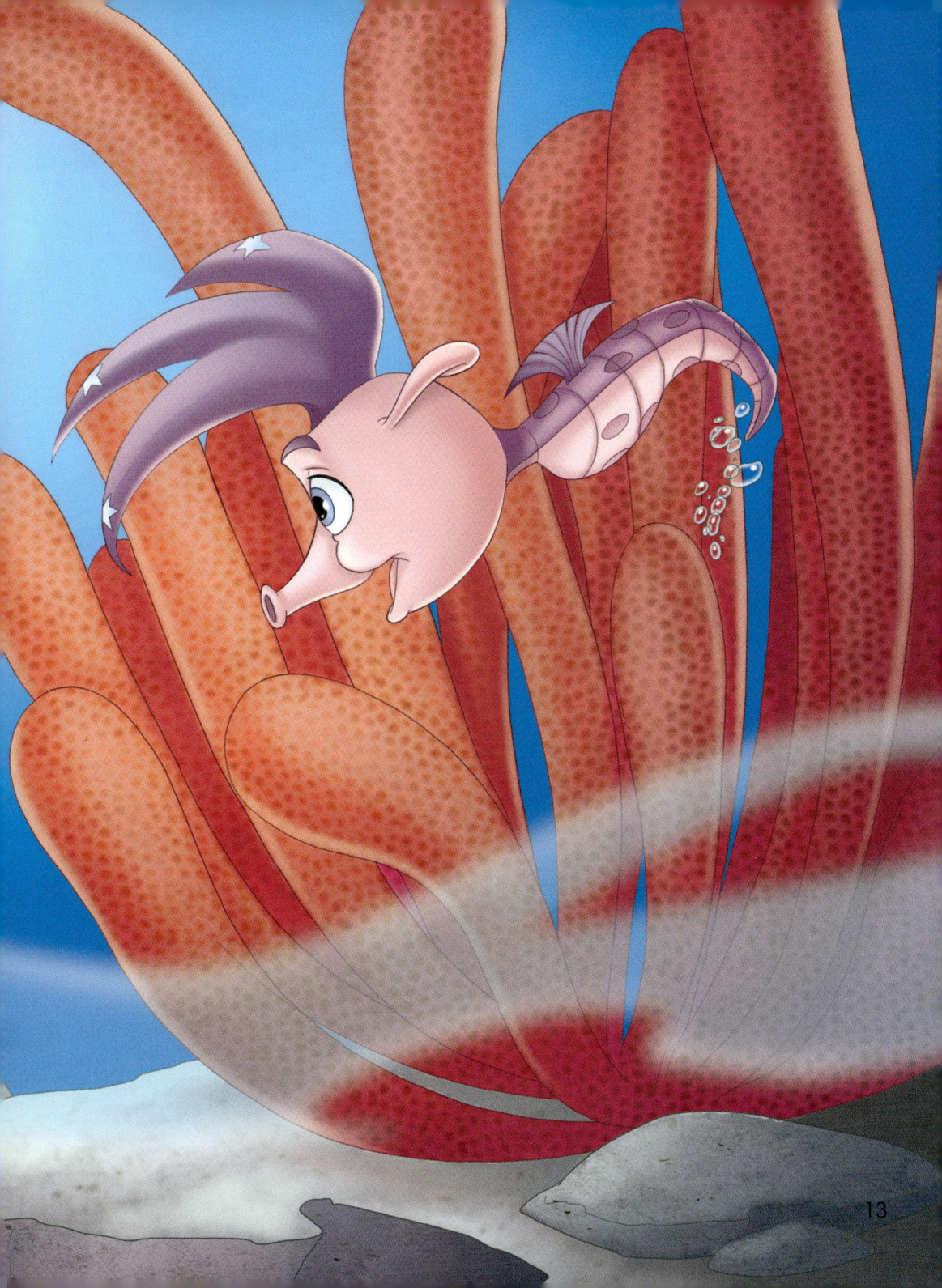

Then Little Sea Horse looked at Spotty Sea Horse.

"Spotty Sea Horse is special," she said.

"And I am special too."

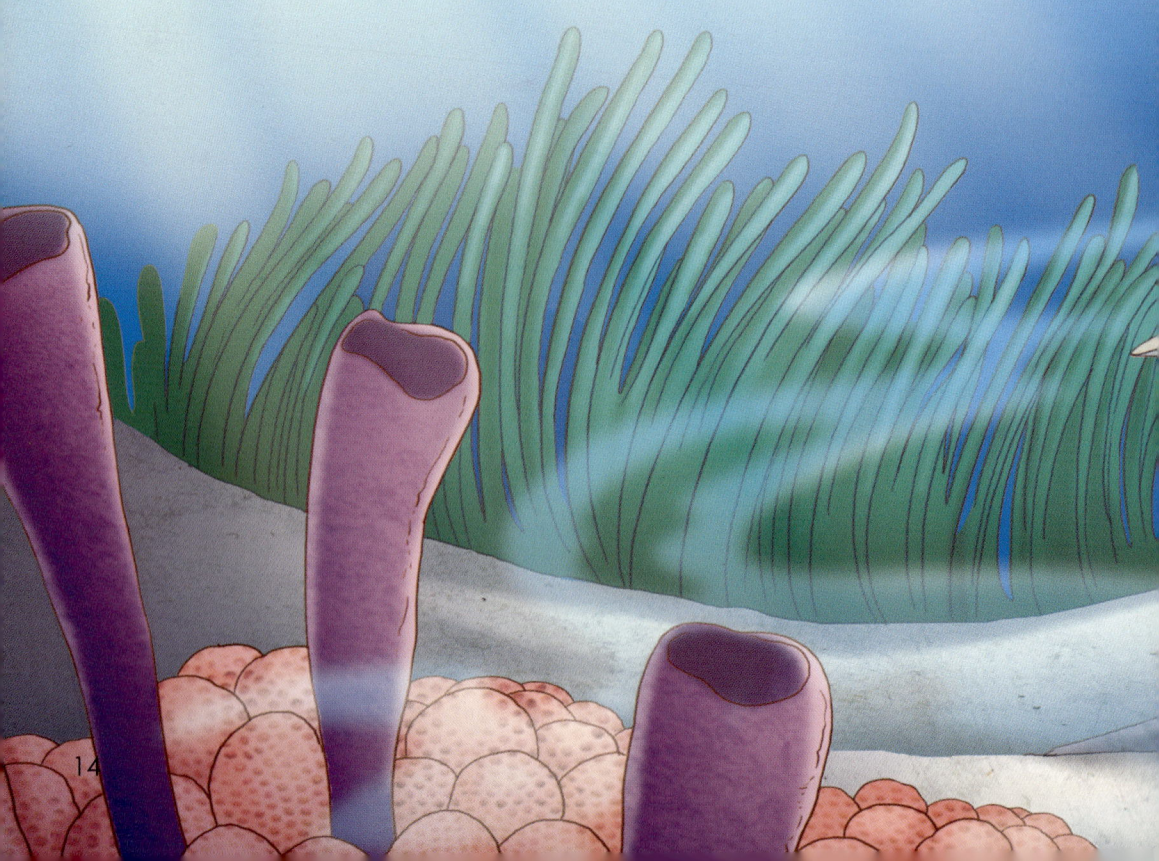